Filthy Games

ANGELA VOX

DEDICATION

To readers who just want mindless smut sometimes, I
hope you enjoy this story.

ACKNOWLEDGMENTS

Ayie, Tin, and Cess, thank you for helping me get here. I wouldn't have had the nerve to do this without you, guys. Ella, thank you for the advice and encouragements. I would also like to give a shout-out to all those YouTube tutorials that helped me figure this thing out. And to all the readers who have been with me for so long now, and to those who just recently found my works, thank you.

FILTHY GAMES

"Want some beer, Mr. Salvatore?"

Raul Salvatore's muscular frame tensed when he heard my voice. The corded muscles of his back tightened as he pushed himself off the hood of the red Mustang, a drop of sweat slithering down his rock-hard bicep as he turned around and faced me.

Breathing deep, I stared back at his cold dark eyes.

How many times had I fantasized cumming around his cock as I stared at those dark stony eyes? How many times had I touched myself moaning his name, imagining his mouth sucking on my nipples, his hardness pounding into my pussy until his semen filled my cunt and dripped down my ass?

Too many times.

It had all started as a harmless crush two years ago when I moved to LA to live with my grandmother.

I became close friends with the teenage girl living next door. I was two years older than Gia, who was also my schoolmate, and we started hanging out at their place.

Then I met him.

My fingers curled tighter around the cold bottle of beer as I stared at the man in front of me.

Raul Alejandro Salvatore.

The man with cold dark eyes, sensual mouth, and godlike body.

Tall, dark, and sinful.

My friend's father.

Yes. Mr. Panty Melting Hot was my friend's dad.

My friend's thirty-six-year-old and very *married* dad.

I threw a glance at Raul's left hand, at the platinum wedding band on his ring finger. The sun glinted off the piece of metal, hitting my eyes for a moment, mocking me, reminding me he was forbidden. Out of reach. And I would burn in Hell for even thinking of it.

I flicked my gaze back to Raul's face as my heart pounded against my rib cage.

Yes. Hell it was for me.

Because I wanted this man.

And I was going to get him.

Tilting his head back, Raul regarded me with a stony expression on his face, making me remember exactly how I felt when I first saw him.

Gia invited me to their house to hang out in their pool that day two years ago. I wore a two-piece white bikini then, laughing and chatting with Gia as we sauntered out of the back patio leading to the pool deck.

Then I saw him.

It had almost been the same scene like the one right now. Raul was leaning under the hood of a vintage sports car, fixing something in the engine. He wore a gray shirt then, too, the fabric fitting across his wide muscular shoulders and strong chest. He had grease stains on his shirt and corded arms, and a line of sweat dampened the back of his shirt. His dark jeans looked buttery soft as they molded his gorgeous ass and the length of his powerful thighs and legs. And when he straightened his large frame and turned toward us, I froze in my tracks.

Because hot damn, the guy was sex on steroids.

Raul had stood there before me, the sun on his back, his mouth unsmiling, his angular jaw rough with five o'clock shadow. His short wavy hair was disheveled, and an image of my fingers grasping those inky strands slammed through my mind.

I had only been seventeen then, but I was not completely innocent. I'd watched stuff online and had a healthy collection of erotic romance novels on my Kindle. And anyone who read erotic romance knew it was the shit. Those things taught you how to give great head among other things. I'd seen loads of gorgeous men in real life, too. My father was a film director after all, and I'd met a lot of hunky actors since I was in diapers.

But nothing had prepared me for the raw animal masculinity of Raul Salvatore.

As I stared up at him back then, more images had burned through my thoughts.

My soft curves pressed against his muscular frame, my pebbled nipples scraping across his chiseled chest, my nails digging into his muscular back, my legs around his waist, our bodies moving, rocking, grinding.

Hot. Sweaty. Dirty.

Groans and slurping wet noises.

Skin to skin.

A pulsing heat flared between my thighs back then just as it did now.

I blinked and slightly shook my head, dispersing the lurid thoughts hazing my mind as I fought the urge to squeeze my thighs together to ease the pressure between them.

That was two years ago, and now I was nineteen. Raul Salvatore didn't look a day older. Or maybe he did. But he only looked hotter. Age only made men like him more fuckable.

"Beer?" I tried to keep my voice as casual as I could despite the thundering of my heart.

Raul didn't respond, but his stony gaze drifted down my curves in a blatant eye-fucking.

My breath stuttered, and I almost dropped the beer in my hand.

I wore the same white bikini I wore that first time I met him two years ago. But it was now two sizes too small. The bikini top could barely hold my 34-C boobs, the plump cheeks of my ass bare—the tiny scrap of thong just enough to cover my mound.

Raul deliberately eyed my pebbled nipples poking through my nylon bikini cups, then his gaze swept down between my thighs, focusing on my plump pussy scarcely concealed by the pad of my white thong.

"Uhm…" I licked my lips, and his gaze snapped back to my face.

Raul's gaze narrowed.

"Gia called," Raul intoned in a voice as icy as his eyes. He turned his attention back to the stuff under the hood of his car, dismissing my presence like some unwanted baggage in his garage. "She's staying with her grandmother tonight. Go back to your house."

Curt. Distant.

He had always been like that to me.

It made my sex throb.

With unsteady legs, I took a step toward Raul and pressed my palm on the frame of the Mustang, leaning over until my breasts almost touched the tensed muscles of his bicep.

His grip tightened around a wrench he was sticking onto some part of the engine, and he turned his head to cut me with a stony glare. The compulsion to step back was overwhelming, but I stood my ground. We were so close the heat of his body licked my skin.

"I know." My voice was reedy. "She called me, too."

Gia and I were supposed to hang out in their house today. But Gia's maternal grandmother called this noon and asked her to go shopping. Gia didn't want to go, but she missed her granny and mother.

Yes, Gia missed her mother.

Because Gia's mother wasn't in the house either…

Mrs. Salvatore had been staying in her mother's house since her fight with Raul a month ago.

It was only me and Raul in the house.

Just that thought made me lightheaded.

And hot.

And achy.

And wet.

So… so… wet.

"Gia gave me keys to your house, and I just thought…"

Raul pushed himself completely off the hood and stepped toward me.

My eyes widened, and I took an involuntary step back

despite myself.

"What did you just think, Angelique?" he asked coolly.

"I…uh…" Blood pounded in my ears and rushed to my head, to my breasts, to the flesh between my thighs. "I…I just…Uhm…"

I hated myself for stuttering, but I couldn't help it. My heart thumped so fast I couldn't think.

I fell back another step as Raul took another step toward me. My naked back bumped against the side of the Mustang, and I jerked back. The metal felt icy against my heated skin.

"Well…Uhm…No one's at my place, so I uhm…"

Raul stopped a few inches away from me, drenching me with his body heat. The air burned between us, and every nerve in my body seemed to pulsate. My senses buzzed as his scent swamped me. He smelled like clean sweat, leather, and a hint of car oil.

Male.

He just smelled so potently male.

He lifted one arm, and the pulse between my legs flared hotter, making me suck in a sharp breath. But Raul only reached for the bottle of beer in my hand.

Dark eyes on me, he raised his large hand gripping the bottle, tipped his head back, and downed the icy liquid.

He watched me through half-lidded eyes as he drank, and I could only stare at him with wide eyes as my heart thumped in my throat. A drop of sweat slinked down his muscled neck, and his strong Adam's apple bobbed with every swallow.

With a last chug, Raul emptied the bottle and placed it on the rolling workbench beside the Mustang. Then he leaned forward, raising his muscular arms and resting both on the roof of the vehicle, caging me between his hard body and the muscle car, blocking out the light and everything else.

"I…"

"Go back to your house, Angelique." He cut me off, but his beer-flavored breath heated my parted lips. His pitiless mouth was inches from mine and I knew that if I lifted my face and parted my lips more, I would taste him on my tongue.

"I don't play games with little girls."

He pushed himself off the car again, and it took my hazy brain a couple of seconds to process what he said.

And when it did, my muscles locked, and panic clawed at my gut.

"Wait!" I gripped his forearm and pulled at him. "I…"

His muscles clenched underneath my palm, and he shot me a murderous glare.

I fought the urge to shrink back. "I want you," I whispered before he could say anything more. "I–I w-want you."

God, I was going to faint.

Raul was the exact opposite. He looked so damn icy he could probably freeze me in a couple more minutes. But his gaze narrowed even more.

Then, the corners of his lips curled, making my belly flutter with apprehension.

"You want me?" he asked in that steely tone.

"I…"

It seemed like a simple direct yes or no question. But there was a dangerous edge in his gaze, a lethal bite in his voice that made my sex clench and my pulse jump with unease.

"I …I do."

He pulled his arm from my grip and took two steps back, shoving his fists in the pockets of his jeans, making the fabric of his shirt stretch across his wide muscular shoulders.

"Fucking an older married man turns you on?"

"W-what?" I stuttered. "N-no! It's not—"

"On your knees," he ordered. "Suck my cock."

W-what?

My mouth fell open, and a derisive sneer curved his sculpted lips at my expression.

"What are you waiting for? You want me? Get on your knees, strip off your clothes and suck me off."

Oh my God.

Blood roared in my ears.

S-suck him off?

So…we're going to do it?

But s-suck him off? Here?

My eyes darted around the spacious garage. The steel doors were up, revealing the interior of the outbuilding to the expansive backyard. The cool wind brushed my skin as the warm afternoon sun pierced through the heavy clouds.

There were CCTVs everywhere.

We were alone on the property, and the tall bamboos surrounding the place served as shield to the outside world. But we were still out in the open. Someone could be sneaking around the high walls and spying on us. Gia and Mrs. Salvatore could even decide to go back and walk in on us right there. There were no locked doors or walls to hide us.

And the CCTV cameras…

And…and—I was a virgin.

Yes, I was a virgin.

I might have watched an embarrassingly huge amount of porn and have masters of theoretical knowledge on giving the best blowjobs and all, but practical experience? Nil.

Practicing blowjobs on a banana and some sex toys didn't count. I hadn't even seen a naked man in real life yet!

I was sure he knew that.

And Raul was ordering me to strip in the middle of his garage, kneel in front of him, and suck his dick like a pro.

Heart in my throat, I stared wide-eyed at Raul again.

His lips curved in a scathing smile as he shook his head. "Don't play games with me, little girl. You can't take me. Go the fuck home and play with your *Barbies*."

He turned and strode off.

My eyes burned.

Little girl.

God, I hated those words.

Was I just a little girl who's trying to play grown up?

My fingers curled into fists, and I drew in a shuddering breath. No, I wasn't.

With trembling fingers, I reached for the strap of my bikini top.

"Should you sit down?" I whispered. "Or should I suck your cock while you're standing?"

Raul froze.

My bikini top dropped to the polished concrete flooring, and my nipples stiffened painfully in the cool air.

Raul turned his large body to face me just as I tugged on the string of my thong. The flimsy fabric floated down to the floor at my feet, and I choked back a whimper at the bite of cold air brushing the creamy lips of my sex.

Quivering, I straightened.

My skin felt so hot as I stood there in the middle of his brightly lit open garage with my ripe breasts, taut nipples, and swollen pussy in full display.

Raul's face was set in stone as he looked at me, and I almost turned and ran.

But I told myself I could do this.

Legs shaking, I stepped toward him.

I saw a nerve pulse in his clenched jaw, and every part of him seemed to be chiseled from granite. He didn't look down at my curves. He kept his gaze on my face with that icy expression.

I stopped when our bodies were practically touching.

I stood there naked and aching; while he stood fully clothed and looking at me with arctic contempt.

But my eyes slid down to the front of his jeans, and my breath shuddered at seeing the large bulge inside.

My pussy throbbed, and my head spun.

He could look at me derisively all he wanted, but his huge erection said it all.

Raul Alejandro Salvatore wanted to fuck me.

Hard.

With shaky hands, I reached for him, pressing my palms on his chiseled abdomen. His steely muscles bunched underneath my palm, and the heat of his skin seeping through his shirt seared my flesh.

God, his muscles were so rigid.

I lifted my wide-eyed gaze at him, and the ruthless look on his handsome face made the heat between my thighs pulsate even more.

My cunt's so wet I was afraid I'd start dripping on his garage floor.

Slowly, I dragged my palm down between his muscular thighs.

I sucked in a harsh breath at the feel of his bulging maleness. He was so thick, so hard. I could feel him throbbing even through his jeans.

My lips parted as my palm massaged his huge erection, and I imagined him pushing inside me, pounding in me, stretching me, forcing my tight little pussy to convulse violently around him.

God, I wanted him.

With shaky breaths, I dropped to my knees in front of him and unbuckled his belt, jerking the strip of leather through the loops. I tugged his jeans and boxers brief down his hips.

And blood rushed to my head as his large cock slipped out of his boxers.

Oh my God.

I had always thought he'd be big, but he was *big*. He was large and swollen, angry veins bulging along the throbbing solid length, the wide cockhead curving up to his navel. His dusky balls looked heavy, and a stream of precum oozed out of the slit of the fat head.

My core clenched, and my inside started to feel so hot and achy I couldn't help but squirm.

Raul's strong fingers fisted in my curly honey brown hair and yanked my head toward his cock. The sting of pain sent a dizzying rush of blood to my head, and I felt more hot wetness trickling down my slit.

"Lick," he ordered.

I fought the urge to rock my hips.

This was it. I was really going to do it.

My breath shuddered as I opened my mouth and darted out my tongue.

And the first hit of his salty clean taste sent saliva pooling in my mouth. A moan ripped out of my throat.

"Fuck." Raul's jaw bunched, and his fingers gripped my curls harder.

The bite of violence made my blood sing, and I opened my mouth wider to rub my tongue on the underside of his shaft, smearing my saliva all over the veiny length. His precum dribbled down his thickness, and I licked it up like cream, slurping the whitish fluid as I suckled on his turgid flesh.

He tasted so good.

Raul's breathing turned ragged, and it spurred me on.

I wrapped my fingers around the weighty length and squeezed, making him grit out another curse. I kept my eyes on his as I rubbed my plump lips and wet tongue up and down the side of his throbbing cock. So hard, so big. I couldn't wait to feel him inside me. My lips closed around a large vein at the wide root and suckled fast.

His nostrils flared, and he fisted my hair. "Suck the tip. And don't fucking use your teeth."

I moaned and rolled my hips.

He was so aggressive and harsh.

Dragging the flat of my tongue up his length, I curled my fingers around the thick root and pumped, but he was so big my fingers couldn't meet. Still squeezing and pumping him, I wrapped my lips around the bulbous cockhead, hollowing out my cheeks as I dragged my plump lips down his engorged shaft.

"Fuck!" His hips bucked and shoved his swollen rod deep into my mouth.

I gasped and my hands flew at his thighs. He was too

big!

But he kept his grip on my hair tight as he pushed and pushed, forcing me to swallow more and more of his massive girth.

I choked on his cock as my plump lips stretched wide around his thickness.

"Breathe slowly through your nose," he ordered.

I could barely hear him through the roar of blood in my ears and the throbbing fire between my legs. He pushed and pushed until my lips were strained wide around the heavy root, my nose practically pressed to his groin, my mouth full of his cock. God, he was huge.

Breathe…breathe…

I tried to remember all my blowjob know-how from all the porn and erotic romance I voraciously consumed, and even the stuff I practiced by myself.

Slowly, my mouth and jaw began to relax.

"That's it," he rasped, praising me as he drove deeper. "Breathe slowly."

His hips started moving, and I had no choice but to obey him. I sucked more and more of him, my tongue massaging every part of him I could.

"Fuck, that's it."

With a grunt, he palmed the back of my head and started fucking my mouth.

I whimpered and dug my fingers into his muscular thighs as he fucked my mouth like he owned it.

Hard, fast and rough. My lips slid up and down his wide shaft as my tongue rasped along the veiny length. My saliva and his salty precum started dribbling down my chin, and the sloppy sound of his dick pushing in and out of my mouth filled my ears.

"Yeah, your mouth feels fucking good," he grunted as he pumped his hips.

I moaned at his praise, and my hips started rolling in time with his thrust. The immense pressure between my legs throbbed in time with every pump of his hips.

I didn't know exactly what I had expected when I went out of the house into his garage wearing that tiny bikini this afternoon.

I did want to seduce him. I had thought maybe I could lure him to bed in one of the guest rooms, get him to finally notice me as a woman, and take my virginity.

But I had never imagined this. Me on my knees in the middle of his garage, my pussy exposed and leaking, my breasts bouncing roughly with every heavy thrust of his cock into my mouth.

It was so dirty. So crude.

Raul Alejandro Salvatore fucking my mouth like I was a common slut.

More cream oozed down my slit, and I moaned around his shaft. Sweat and precum dripped down between my swollen breasts, and I wanted to rub them on my skin and squeeze my boobs.

"Fuck," he groaned, gripping my hair harshly as he drove his cock into the back of my throat.

I gagged, but he only tightened his grasp on my hair.

"You love sucking my cock, little girl?" Raul taunted as he eased his shaft out a little bit.

My breasts heaved as I looked up at him, and the vicious look on his stunning face made me whimper. He looked so savagely aroused it made my whole body tremble. I tightened my plump lips around his throbbing thickness, hollowing out my cheeks further to increase my suction.

"Fuck yeah!" he snarled and pistoned his hips to shove himself back into my mouth.

I was more prepared this time and took it obediently. I gurgled around his cock but didn't gag. I breathed through my nose as my whole body seemed to vibrate. I was so wet. The flesh between my thighs was so swollen. So heavy. My nipples were turgid and aching. How could I be so horny with just sucking him off?

Sliding one hand between his muscular thighs, I cupped his hefty balls and squeezed.

"Fuck!" His hips lurched forward, driving himself down my throat again.

My boobs quaked from the force, and tears stung my eyes, but my pussy only contracted viciously.

"Swallow," he grunted.

I had no choice but to obey as jets of heated fluid flooded my throat.

On and on and on…

He kept thrusting, kept pumping my throat with his cum.

I swallowed and swallowed until there was no more.

"Good girl," he rasped as he tugged at my hair, pulling my head away, my swollen lips sliding away from his length.

I gasped for air, my breasts heaving. His cum had dribbled down my chin and upper breasts, making them sticky.

He was still rock-hard.

I looked up at him, and the feral glint in his eyes made me moan.

"You look so fucking good like that. Your fuckable lips and tits smeared with my cum."

With that, he pulled at my hair and forced me to stand up. My knees buckled, and I stumbled onto him.

My curves pressed onto his muscled body, but he pushed me back and spun me around, pressing my front onto the side of the Mustang. I cried out and jerked back from the searing coldness of the metal against my hot skin. But Raul's heavy palm struck the cheek of my ass.

"Oh, God!" I jolted and clutched at the car.

"Ass out," he barked.

His calloused palms squeezed the plump globes of my ass, and the stinging heat penetrated deep between my thighs. I moaned out loud and rocked my hips to push my ass onto his palms. It felt so good.

"You like that." His large palm smacked the cheek of my ass again.

Shuddering, I begged, "Please…"

"Hm…" he purred, pressing a hand on my naked back, pushing my front against the car as his other hand gripped my hips and pulled my ass toward him.

"Spread your legs wide." He slapped the inside of my thigh. "Show me your cunt."

He was so harsh. So filthy.

My pussy gushed more cream.

Jutting out my buttocks, I held onto the roof of the Mustang and arched my back, widening my stance, rocking my hips, and presenting him my creamy swollen sex.

Raul growled. "Fuck, your cunt's drooling."

Without warning, he palmed my mound and squeezed.

My breath wheezed, and my legs shook. I rocked my hips in his palm to make him touch me more. He obliged, spreading my engorged folds apart, then he shoved thick fingers deep into my opening.

"Oh, fuck!" My body quaked, and my fingers clawed at the roof of the car.

My slick flesh constricted around him, but he only screwed his rough fingers deeper, stretching my fleshy muscles, burying his digits to the third knuckle inside me.

"You've got such a juicy little cunt."

He pushed and twisted his fingers inside, chafing my sensitive vaginal walls. My insides quivered, and sobs tore out of me. My legs gave out, but Raul's brawny arm harshly gripping my waist kept me up.

"Such a tight little cunt."

His brutal fingers screwed in and out, in and out, stretching me, rubbing me, inflaming my taut flesh until my pussy was a sopping wet mess. Copious juices dribbled down my shaking inner thighs, and sloppy wet noises mixed with my throaty whimpers filled the air. The tangy scent of sex rose from my body.

"You hear that noise, hm?" he taunted in my ear. "Your cunt's so fucking dirty."

He curled his thick fingers inside me and pumped so fast my vagina shook.

"Oh, God! Oh, God!" My hips bucked and I couldn't stop shaking.

"You like that, huh?" His fingers pumped faster as his other palm on my waist skimmed up my rib cage to my breast and squeezed the ripe mound.

My whole body was on fire.

He finger-fucked me the way he had fucked my mouth. No sweet touches, no soft tender caresses, no teasing strokes. It was fast, hard, and brutal.

I felt a sharp sting of something steely abrading the fleshy walls of my sex, and my core spasmed and creamed at the realization that it was his wedding ring.

My vaginal walls contracted furiously and I screamed.

"Such a dirty little slut," he groaned in my ear as his calloused fingers continued pumping in and out of my convulsing sex. "You feel my wedding ring inside your greedy little cunt, hm?"

Whimpering, I rocked my hips helplessly on his hand.

Deep, deep, deep. I wanted him deep.

"Fuck," he growled, and I felt his hot wet tongue laving the side of my neck. His other big hand continued palming and squeezing my aching boobs.

"Raul…" I sobbed.

"You want me to fuck you, Angelique?" he rasped in my ear.

"Yes," I whimpered. "Please…yes!"

His lips suckled the side of my neck. "This is going to be nothing but a hard fuck. Don't get ideas."

He pulled his fingers out of me, and his open palm slapped my sopping wet slit.

I keened and jolted at how brutal he was.

Then he was gripping my hips again, jutting out my ass even more, and the swollen head of his hardness pressed stiff into my taut opening.

I didn't get the chance to prepare myself. The broad crest of his cock pushed into my snug entrance and ripped deep into my pussy in one savage stroke.

"Ah!" My body rocked forward, and my fingers clawed at anything I could reach.

"Fuck!" Raul's fingers dug into my hips as his own hips gave another brutal thrust to drive the last heavy inch of his shaft into my quivering hole.

My vaginal muscles clamped around his massive length, and all my senses went into overdrive. The enormous pressure between my thighs was like nothing I'd ever felt before. He was so rigid and big that I couldn't breathe. I grasped onto the side of the Mustang, onto the roof, onto anything.

"So fucking tight."

That was the only warning I got before he withdrew from my clenching depth then slammed his shaft balls deep inside me again.

My body staggered, and my cries rent the air.

Raul only grunted and strengthened his bruising grip on my hips, then started pounding into my pussy with savage force.

My eyes rolled to the back of my head.

My clit swelled with fire.

My core tightened and tightened with every bruising pound of his cock.

I moaned and whimpered as his rod pummeled my pussy.

It felt so good.

Our bodies slapped together, my ripe breasts flushing against the side of the Mustang, my body lurching forward with every ruthless thrust of his hips. The lurid slurping sound of my slobbering pussy being fucked by his cock was loud in my ears.

"Oh, please…please…please…"

"Such a hot little cunt," he snarled in my ear as he rotated his hips and ground his large rod into my sex. "I'm gonna fuck you anytime I want to."

He adjusted behind me and started drilling faster into my fleshy hole. My body spasmed, and I tried to find purchase on the Mustang to move, but I could only sob and hold on as his hips pistoned and drove his cock into me in fast brutal strokes.

I was so full. So crammed. He stretched me so much, and the burning fullness radiated a sharp ache throughout my core.

He growled in my ear and rolled his hips, screwing his thickness pitilessly into my tightness.

The hot pressure exploded in my core, and I screamed.

Raul cursed and slammed deeper into me. His fingers found my clit and furiously rubbed the engorged bundle of nerves.

"Oh, God!" My whole body turned rigid as the jagged blade of heat ripped throughout my system again.

He cursed, and his other hand gripped my chin and turned my face toward him. He fused his mouth to mine, his tongue thrusting deep into my mouth. I whimpered and sobbed as my body vibrated with sensory overload. His hand dropped down to my breast and squeezed hard as he continued pounding into my cunt.

I had always dreamed of my first time to be with him. I had imagined it would be rough. But I had never dreamed it would be like this. In the middle of the garage, standing up, him still in his clothes and fucking me roughly from behind with my boobs pressed flat against the side of his Mustang.

Yet there I was, whimpering in his mouth as his hips ground against my ass, screwing his cock deeper into my sex as I cum deliriously around him. He was so deep I could feel his balls flushed taut against my clit.

"You want my cum inside you?" he rumbled against my mouth.

"Yes!" I pushed my hips back and rotated it in time with his grinding. "Oh, God…"

The delicious burning of my flesh stretching wide around his thickness made me cum again.

"Fuck!" With his muscular arm wound harsh around my

waist, he kept me immobile as he jackhammered his hips against my ass.

The heavy pounding into my sex shot me into another delirious storm of fire. My vision turned white as my body shuddered uncontrollably.

"Fuck, fuck, fuck!" He swelled impossibly thicker, and he drilled into me harsh and deep. Blasts of hot semen flooded my cunt.

The hot fluid bathed my walls and inflamed my already tender sex.

Every throbbing pump felt like a heavy thrust, his thickening rod stretching my pulsating muscles to a fevered ache.

I moaned and sobbed, my hips shaking, rocking, my pussy contracting around his cock to get more of his cum.

"Fuck," he rasped against my neck as he continued pumping.

Panting, I slanted my head to catch his lips. He obliged me and covered my mouth with his.

Our tongues mated and tangled as he pumped me full of semen until I could feel the hot fluid leaking out at the side of my sex despite his large maleness tightly buried deep inside me. I moaned at the feel of his cum dripping down my inner thighs.

Slowly, our breaths evened out. But my flesh continued to spasm around his shaft.

From somewhere in the garage, a phone rang.

Raul groaned and buried his face in the crook of my shoulder.

Panting, I also let out a groan.

The phone kept ringing.

I laughed and gently slid my fingers through his disheveled hair. "You need to get that."

He groaned again. "I don't want to." His muscular arms constricted around my waist.

His heavy length jerked inside me, and I gasped. He was starting to grow thicker inside me again.

"You broke character," I teased, wriggling my ass.

"Did I?" He rocked his hips, lazily thrusting his engorged shaft inside me again.

"Yes," I moaned, rocking my hips back. "You're not supposed to kiss me!"

"Right." To show me how much he didn't give a fuck, his fingers gripped my chin and pulled my face for a rough kiss.

I moaned and arched my back.

But I turned my face away from his. I grinned at my husband.

Yes, my husband.

Raul Alejandro Salvatore was my husband.

We're in our garage.

"Tomorrow, you'll be my Physics teacher, and I'll be your student, okay?"

Laughing, he shook his head at me. "You and your dirty games."

My own laughter rang in the spacious garage, and I kissed my husband again.

We've been married for a year now, and we'd been playing these dirty games since we were girlfriend and boyfriend.

And no, I wasn't nineteen, though I wasn't that much older. I turned twenty-two last month, while Raul was thirty this year. I did have a babyface, though, and I usually got carded in bars and clubs. I was kind of annoyed with it when I was younger. But now I realized it made dirty role-playing games like this so much more fun.

Our families had been long-time friends, and we had been in a relationship since I was eighteen.

At least four times a month, we would do these little games just for fun. I loved it. And with the way Raul's hardness moved heavily inside me again, I knew he loved it, too.

We'd probably play this until we were old and gray.

"I love you," he murmured against my mouth.

The corners of my lips curved, and I pressed a sweet kiss on his sculpted mouth. "And I love you."

~THE END~

22

ABOUT THE AUTHOR

Angela Vox loves steamy romance stories with happily ever afters. Reading is her first and greatest love and always will be.